A STEP BAC

The

Murray Barber P. I.

Case

By

Julie Burns Sweeney

Copyright: 2017

Published by: Lulu.com

ISBN: 978-0-244-91166-9

CHAPTER ONE

Murray half opened his eyes. Someone was talking to him. The young sounding woman's voice was coming from across the other side of the bedroom, a bedroom which didn't look familiar... but somehow did? The voice didn't sound familiar either. It wasn't Jenny... in fact it didn't sound like Michelle neither. Had he got himself very drunk the previous night? Murray couldn't remember. Just then a very pretty blonde strolled into his vision wearing just her bra and panties and holding a pair of dark green cord trousers in her hands.

".... Are you listening to a word I'm saying?" she asked sweetly.

"Erm... sorry, I'm not awake yet." Murray humoured her. Maybe he wasn't awake yet and this was just a pleasant dream? Though it somehow felt very real. He was feeling confused and the young lady was about to add to his confusion.

"Well, you'd better wake up now. You promised to drop me off at the market square so that I won't be late for work. Some of us have to work Saturdays!" She pulled on knee length socks and the cords and then grabbed a frilly white blouse, covered in tiny orange flowers, from the chair in the corner of the room. "Come on Adam! Up!"

'Adam'? Murray felt dazed but could only think to play along until he could remember what had happened the night before. Maybe he had told her that was his name? He still couldn't place when or where they had met.

He struggled out of bed and bashfully clutched a pair of jeans from the floor and headed out the door and into the bathroom which he found directly opposite. There things became even less clear, for as he glanced in the mirror he found a strange face staring back at him. Dark shoulder length hair and FACIAL hair? What was going on? Was he having an odd out of body experience? An 'in someone else's body' experience? The only good thing about this stranger he could see in the mirror was that he looked a few years younger than Murray's thirty years. Twenty-four maybe? Maybe he did look familiar? Ok, this had to be some kind of weird dream so he was just going to enjoy it until someone woke him up! He washed, no need to shave it seemed, and dressed. Finding a set of keys and a wallet in the jeans pocket, he took a moment to find out who he was. Adam Cannon-Leigh, born 14th March 1951. Ok. 1951? Not as young as he thought? He then glanced at the keys in his hand. Ford? No button on the fob to unlock or disable an alarm so must be a basic or old model? No doubt he would find out when he went outside. He turned and stepped back into the bedroom where he found his new friend brushing her long hair and tying it into a loose ponytail.

  "Ready?" she asked as she grabbed a brown leather shoulder bag from the end of the bed.

  "Whenever you are." A coffee would have been nice but maybe you just don't need to eat or drink in dreams? She kissed him full on the lips before she walked out through the door. He got a clear taste of cherry, this was the weirdest dream he'd ever had!

Outside, he found himself on a street of Victorian terraced houses. It seemed either him or her, he hadn't yet remembered her name, had a bedsit on the first floor of number 17. She was waiting for him next to a navy blue Ford Cortina, a classic from the early seventies! Murray wouldn't call himself a 'petrol-head' but he did know a bit about cars, just like most men! He climbed in and started up the engine, it started on the first turn of the key which made him smile, and as 'Miss X' climbed in next to him, Murray stared out of the window at his surroundings. Furrows appearing on his brow as he took in the other few cars in the street. They were

all classics. A Hillman Avenger, Vauxhall Viva, another two Cortina's and an Escort and at the far end of the row he could swear he could see a Morris Marina. Murray sat for a moment thinking about the clothes they were wearing, about the fittings in the room, about the blanket and sheets on the bed which he had slept in. Somehow he felt completely calm. But this was certainly odd even for a dream....
It was a clear day, the sun being quite high in the sky. Summer Murray assumed? He wasn't sure how, part of the dream most probably, but he knew exactly how to get to the market. Pretty Miss X had chatted away enabling him to learn that she worked at the Bookies around the corner from the market and that he, Adam, was actually in a relationship with her boss's daughter Janet. Maybe this dream

was a 'wake-up call' about his own behaviour regarding long-term girlfriend Jenny and recent bit-on-the-side Michelle? The enjoyment he had been feeling started to feel a little tainted.

The market clock showed two minutes to ten. Miss X jumped out of the car saying she was about to be late. She stopped briefly to smile at him through the open passenger window and wish him a good day-off and to be careful what he said if he came in to place any bets. Murray replied with an 'I'm always careful!' which surprised him but he was getting into the role of Adam now. He watched her disappear off into the busy market before deciding to find a parking spot and go in hunt of a coffee shop, maybe a good old fashioned market cafe? Whether by his own imagination or by some other method, Murray found that very same 'old fashioned market cafe' and headed inside for a well-needed cuppa.

He was just sat gazing out of the window at the busy stall-holders, enjoying the rich taste of full cream milk in his coffee when he realized he was being waved at by another young lady. A dark-haired, tall girl wearing a long yellow summer dress and navy cardigan, came bounding in the cafe door and planted a full-on kiss on his lips before flopping down in the seat opposite him.

"You're in town early Darling?" Murray wondered whether or not this was Janet? It was probably a safe bet to say 'yes' considering that kiss but he decided to play safe and refrain from using any names.

"It's a lovely day! Silly to waste my day off. Where are you off too?" he smiled waving towards the waitress for a second cup for his guest.

"On my way to see Daddy. He wants me to go and pick out something for Mummy's birthday. There's enough staff in that place for him to go and get something himself but I just don't think he trusts either of them."

"Maybe he doesn't trust his own judgement? About the present I mean."

"Oh you are sweet Adam. I'm very lucky to have a man like you." The waitress brought the coffee over. "We are still going to Freddie's party later aren't we? It's only that I've just seen the most wonderful dress over on Danny's stall. Maybe you could treat me?" she had leant forward and was making

11

fluttering eyes at him. Murray sipped his coffee and tried to think like a 1970's man.

"If you show me which one, maybe I'll think about it?"

"Oh you Darling! Danny knows which one. Could you drop it off into Daddy's for me so I have it for tonight?" She took a gulp of her drink and stood up. "I'd better go else Daddy will wonder where I am." She kissed him once again and then paused before she left. "What time will you pick me up later?"

"Erm... what time's the party?"

"Never starts before ten!"

"I'll pick you up at ten then."

"Lovely!" she beamed and then ran out of the door before Murray realized he had no idea where he was meant to pick her up from. Hopefully this dream would also enable him to find his way to Janet, and the party, just like it had helped him find the market?

Having finished his coffee, Murray wandered around the square looking for a dress stall. From behind him a man's voice called out the name Adam. Turning, he spotted a man of similar age to himself beckoning him over. The fair-haired man was wearing a red polo shirt and flared jeans and was holding a newspaper in his hands.

"Janet wants this one." He smiled. "I take it you're buying it for her?"

"Apparently so." Murray replied glancing more at the newspaper than the dress. "How much is it?" he asked.

"Sort it out later mate. You see Liverpool have

made Paisley their new manager? Fifty-five he is! Mind you that is five years younger than Shankly but he'd been with the club for fifteen years!"

"Mmm." Murray wasn't sure about Liverpool F.C. history but he was pretty sure they won the F.A. cup in 1974 with Bill Shankly as their manager? He was trying to see the date at the top of the paper.

"Still, long as they keep Keagan they should be alright. You wanna take this now mate?"

"Er, yeah please. She asked me to drop it off in the bookies with her Dad." Ah, Saturday 27th July 1974.

"He seems to like you. Better make sure he don't find out about you and Melanie!" Murray cast a quick glance at Danny. Was Melanie the name of Miss X? "She'd certainly be out of a job and you'd never be seen again!" Danny was laughing but

Murray wasn't sure it was so funny. "Anyway, catch you at Freddie's later? Best parties in town!"

Murray took the now bagged dress and headed back across the market square in the direction of the Bookies. As he pushed open the door and walked in he was met by Janet's Daddy shouting from the door behind the counter which looked like it led into an office. He was a large balding man wearing a shirt and waist-coat which was unbuttoned. He stopped and looked at Murray as he walked in the door.

"You seen Melanie?" he shouted. Murray wasn't sure what to say at first. Had he been found out? "She's not turned up for work. Not like her at all." Murray stood with his mouth open. He had only dropped her off around the corner not more than half an hour ago. Where could she have possibly disappeared to? He couldn't say anything so he just shook his head and lifted the bag with Janet's dress in over the counter. The other man behind the counter was middle-aged and was busy writing on a white-board, a cigarette smoking away between his lips. He seemed little interested in the whereabouts of his co-worker.

"Do you want me to go look for her?" Murray asked.

"Can do. But if she's not here by eleven, she hasn't got a job anymore!" Daddy turned and shut himself in his office taking Janet's dress with him. Murray looked to the other man.

"You didn't see her on your way in then?" The man didn't answer at first, just drew on his cigarette and raised his eyebrows at Murray before glancing over at the office door.

"You want me to tell him who's car she climbed out of?"

"So where did she go?" Murray asked not wanting to get into a conversation about the previous night.

"Dunno. Didn't stop to watch the whole show. You should have a better idea than me." He then turned back to his board and continued writing up the odds for the coming races at Sandown and Newmarket. Murray walked back out into the market square and stared around him. There wasn't any sign of Melanie in her green cords and flowered blouse amongst the mass of morning shoppers.

He found his way back over to Danny's stall. He was busy giving a couple of girls a lot of fancy talk about how gorgeous they would look in one of his many dresses. Murray waited until Danny had successfully completed his sale and then caught his eye and asked him if he had seen Melanie walk across the square?

"Yeah, I saw her. Asked her if she was going to Freddie's tonight. Said she might but she'll have to watch it if you have too much to drink, you might forget who you're with!"

"Hmm. Which way did she go?"

"To work. Why?"

"She didn't get there....."

"Murray! Murray! Are you alright Murray?" It was his Aunt Pam's voice that was drifting into his head. Slowly Murray opened his eyes and roused from his slumber. He wasn't in bed however, as his Aunt peered down at him with a worried expression upon her face, Murray found himself staring up at her loft hatch which was open. He went to sit up but a throbbing pain shot between his eyes. He lay back down for a moment and then glanced around him. He was laying on Pam's landing with a ladder on the floor one side of him and a man dressed as a paramedic on the other. Pam had one hand on his chest and held his hand with the other. "Oh, you're alright!" she sounded relieved. "I just heard this almighty crash and when I ran up here you were flat out on the floor. Out cold!"

"Uhh, what happened....?"

CHAPTER TWO

After some convincing, the paramedic was happy for Murray to stay at his Aunt's and not take the trip to hospital. Nothing seemed to be broken and Murray was able to remember climbing the ladder in the search of a box of books which Pam wanted to donate to the local school's table-top sale. He had lost his footing and fallen, knocking himself out on the bannister. His only promise was not to drive for twenty-four hours which meant he was going to be staying with Aunt Pam overnight.

They now sat at the large kitchen table. Murray was eating tinned soup accompanied by one of Pam's home-baked crusty rolls. She had decided that he shouldn't have anything too heavy in case he took a turn for the worse overnight. He had laughed at her but not in a nasty way and it was as they sat there that he had decided to tell her about the dream he had experienced while 'out cold' on her landing.

"…. it was so vivid. Every detail, even the taste of cherry when she kissed me in the morning."

"It does sound odd. I wonder what made you dream about 1974, that was way before you were even born."

"Something about it didn't feel like a dream Aunt." He noticed she was giving him a sideways look. He had to admit he did sound a little nuts. "Besides, how can I dream about a time I've never experienced?"

"Come on Murray, you've had an education. You've

seen plenty of old tv programmes. It's not that much of a stretch of the imagination. You'll be telling me it's a past life next!" she laughed again as she stood up and refilled the kettle at the sink.

"Hello you two, haven't seen you for a while."

"Aunty Pammy! You're looking good! Alright there Murray my man?"

Murray held his spoon mid-air and glanced around the empty kitchen. The voice of the late Ali had flowed from somewhere near the fridge.

"Ali?" Murray asked "And you here too Rita?"

"Yes, I'm here. Thought we'd find you back home by now, you staying the night?" Rita's spiritual tones came from the other side of the table.

"I'm stuck here for the night! Nearly killed myself climbing into the loft! Fell off the ladder and knocked myself out."

"Didn't think you were ready for this side of life yet Murray mate! And saying you're stuck here isn't very nice man!"

"No it's not is it! Thankyou Murray." His Aunt was mocking.

"I didn't mean it like that Aunt. I suppose you're going to tell these two about my dream now?"

"What dream's this?" Rita asked with interest.

"He's had a very vivid dream about life in the seventies and two very pretty girls!"

"Oh, one of those dreams! Don't think we want to know about that!" Now Ali was laughing too. Murray felt he was being ganged up on, becoming their amusement for the evening.

"Fine. I won't talk about it. I'm going to take a bath

and go to bed."

"Oh, don't be like that Murray, we don't mean it." His Aunt placed a mug of coffee on the table next to him. "It was a very detailed dream and being set before his time does make it quite odd." Pam, who could not only hear the dead but see them as well, was focused on the chair opposite Murray. "It was not so much that though was it Murray, it was more the fact that this poor girl had disappeared and then we brought you round before you found out what happened to her..."

"Mmm. That was frustrating, not knowing if she'd just wandered off or if something nasty had happened to her."

"Surely if it was just a dream it doesn't really matter? Can't you add an ending when you go to bed tonight?"

"Maybe Rita. But... I don't know, I'm probably just feeling odd after the fall but... well, it just felt so real!"

"I said, maybe he's experiencing a past life!" The laugh was back in Pam's voice but the other two didn't answer.

"What?" Not being able to see either Ali or Rita, Murray wondered what 'looks' he was missing out on.

"Well..." Rita started hesitantly. "... It would be very unusual. It's extremely rare for anything like that to happen."

"Ok." Murray got to his feet and placed his empty bowl into the dishwasher. "You lot can continue to discuss my sanity, I'm going for a bath now. If I'm not out in an hour call the ambulance back, I've probably fallen unconscious again!"

While both the living and deceased carried on with their mockery in the kitchen, Murray bathed and then retreated to Pam's spare room where he pulled out his laptop. It had crossed his mind that maybe Janet and Melanie in some way represented Jenny and Michelle? Like some form of guilty conscience playing games with his head? He just needed to check and see if there ever had been an Adam Cannon-Leigh born in March 1951, even if it was only to put his mind at rest. He searched the birth records...

"Bugger me!" He sat back and stared at the screen. Yes, there had really been such a man. So Murray's next step was to try and trace him. He must have spent a good fifteen to twenty minutes trying different sites but there was not a trace of him anywhere. Again Murray sat back but this time he slumped. Maybe it was just a coincidence?

He heard a creak on the stairs and his Aunt's voice call out to see if he wanted some cocoa? He got up and opened his door.

"Sure Aunt." he called. "And you can stop laughing now, I've found a birth entry for Adam Cannon-Leigh!"

His Aunt had stopped on the stair.

"Really?" she asked staring up at him.

"Yep." he answered as he peered over the bannister and followed her down. "So tell me, how did I make that name up?"

"Well, maybe there is something in it then? Rita!" she called ahead into the kitchen, the two ghosts were still around. "This Adam guy really lived. What do you make of that?"

"Wow! Fancy that. I suppose there is the possibility you were him in your last life?" Rita's voice still came from the table. Murray sat himself down where he assumed he was next to her. He glanced to his right.

"Can't find any trace of where he's living now though."

"Err, Murray my man, if he was you then he must have died." Ali's voice came from the head of the table on Murray's left.

"Death records?" Murray jumped up again and ran back upstairs to grab his laptop. He returned

28

downstairs already typing into the search bar. "Oh bugger me!" he spoke in barely more than a whisper as he placed the laptop gently onto the table. Pam placed the mugs down next to it and stared at the screen.

"27th July 1974?" she looked at Murray puzzled.

"That was the day of my dream...."

CHAPTER THREE

Murray didn't sleep well that night. He tossed and turned with his mind racing. The only detail they had managed to find about Adam's death was that it was an 'accidental' death. He still wasn't sure if this was just some kind of mind game or whether or not he actually believed in reincarnation? Ali and Rita had mentioned it happening to others before and Murray had just accepted what they had said without much thought, but it felt very different when they were talking about it having happened to him. He had never considered that he may have lived before. He came to the decision that he wouldn't come to any decision about it until he knew what had happened to Adam. And what had happened to Melanie also...

Rita and Ali had finally disappeared off at about midnight. They said that they would find out anything they could but, as usual, wouldn't make any promises. It was possible that Jeff might be able to find something on the C.I.D. system, maybe Melanie had been reported missing? It would certainly help if she had as Murray never found out her full name during his dream. He just knew the date. During his fitful rest he had tried to think about other avenues he could search but his head hurt and felt like it was shut up inside a box so he had given up thinking. So until morning, he just had to wait....

When morning finally came Murray let his Aunt fill him with a full-English breakfast before insisting on heading home. He wanted to get hold of Jeff and see if he could search the official records. Pam let him go on the promise that he called her as soon as he got in so that she knew he had made it home safely. She also wanted to call Jenny, Murray's girlfriend, and ask her to stay with him for the day but Murray hadn't told her yet what had happened to him and he didn't want to worry her. He told his Aunt he'd invite Jenny over for the evening instead.

As he drove home he wondered how he would explain his dream to Jenny? She still had no idea about his being able to hear ghosts. She would think he was nuts if he told her he thought he had been reincarnated. The drive was clearing his mind so he started working out a plan. First he would call Jeff and set him on the official records. Then he would search the newspaper archives. If Melanie had been reported missing maybe it made the local papers? And then what about Adam himself? Had he had any family? He could check for relatives, they may even still be alive?

The only other job Murray had for the day was to

collect and check his cameras which he had installed in the flat that Mr Lee Woodley rented for his 'mistress'. He was convinced that she was cheating on him and using the very flat which HE was paying for as a meeting place. Well, if she was entertaining anyone else, besides the man cheating on his own wife with her, it should be on film. The cameras had been in place for a week now.

Once back indoors, Murray made himself a coffee and sat himself down at the computer desk. He first sent Jenny a text asking if she fancied a curry later. A text came back immediately saying she'd call him when she was on her way, about seven-ish? He was then able to call his Aunt with a clear conscience and tell her he was home safe and sound. With all that done he was then able to turn his mind to

Adam Cannon-Leigh. He dialled Jeff's number.

"Alright mate?"

"Hello Murray. What can I do for you?" Jeff was sounding cheerful considering he was at that stage where every phone call he received could be from his wife, Kate, counting contractions and demanding to be got to hospital.

"How's Kate?" Murray thought he had better ask.

"All quiet at the moment. Apparently the baby can go quite still just before the onslaught of the birth so she's checking the timing of all movements! Football match was still in full swing when I left home a couple of hours ago so I think we're safe today!"

"The wait must be killing you! Anyway, sorry to bother you but can I ask a favour?"

"I take it that's why you called?"

"Could you check the missing person reports from July or August 1974?"

"1974? Dare I ask why?" Jeff sounded surprised.

"I know! Here I go again. If I tried to explain it all to you you'd think I'd finally lost it."

"Try me."

"Ok... I fell and knocked myself out yesterday at my Aunt Pam's, anyhow during my blackout I had the weirdest dream ever.."

"Dream?"

"Yeah. I know but let me finish. In this dream I was this guy Adam and he had two girlfriends one of which, Melanie, went missing. Or at least I think she did? I came round before I found out..."

"You did say this was a dream Murray?"

"Yes I know, but listen.. when I looked up this guy, Adam, he really existed! And what's more, he died the very day of my dream. 27th July 1974."

"Hang on. Let me get my head round this." There was a pause before Jeff continued. "You get a knock on the head and you have a strange dream about a guy who dies and a girl that goes missing and you now want to know if that girl really went missing?"

"Sort of, yes." Murray knew he wasn't sounding sane. "It was a very vivid dream. And when I found that this Adam was a real person it was just a step to find out about the girl. I didn't dream this guy dying but his death record says he died that same day."

"It all sounds a bit fantastic but I'll go with you for now, as it's you! What about Sonny and Cher? Can they help?"

"It's Ali and Rita! They laughed at first but they won't deny that it could be a past life. And please don't say anything about that, I'm still trying to get my own head around the possibility."

"I don't think I'm going to say anything! What's this girl's name?"

"I only know her first name, Melanie. I'd say she was about twenty? There abouts anyhow. The date was Saturday 27th July 1974."

"Ok, hang on...." Murray could hear Jeff tapping away on his keypad. He himself was searching the name Cannon-Leigh on his own computer. "Well...."

"What?" Murray waited for Jeff to continue.

"Well I never! There's an open case on a missing

girl by the name of Melanie Foskett, double 't'. Age twenty-one, reported missing by her mother, Catherine, on Sunday 28th July 1974. Missing since the Saturday morning when she never arrived at work. Worked at Proctor Bookmakers, Market Street, here in town. Does any of this sound like your dream?"

"Yes." Murray was sat with his mouth open. It was frighteningly similar.

"Oh God!" Jeff interrupted. "Do you know the full name of this Adam guy?"

"Cannon-Leigh." Murray held his breath.

"The last people to see her were Adam Cannon-Leigh and Danny Williams. Adam never made a statement as he died on the Saturday.... Murray this is amazing!" Murray was silent on the other end of the phone. He felt like this could still be part of his 'dream', it was all too weird. "Murray?"

"Yeah, sorry, I'm here. It is really weird isn't it?"

"I'll get this report printed off. You about today?"

"Err, until lunchtime then I've got some equipment to pick up."

"Right, give me an hour and I'll pop over."

"Thanks Jeff. You're a mate."

"No worries."

With the call ended Murray just sat for a few minutes trying to get his head around the whole situation. He started to wonder if there was a reason why he should be experiencing this now? His mind flicked back to the initials J and M. Then he decided he had enough to deal with without imagining spiritual conspiracies as well. So Melanie was also a real person once. And she had gone missing just like in his dream. He felt a pang inside his chest. He knew he was going to have to find her... alive or dead.

He focused back on the computer screen in front of him. Adam had a brother? Or possibly a cousin or uncle? Mr J. Cannon-Leigh still lived in town. Murray jotted down the address and dialled the number on the screen. He had no idea what he was going to say.

"Hello?" It was a woman's voice.

"Err, hello, could I speak to Mr Cannon-Leigh please?"

"I'm afraid he's not here. Who's calling?"

"Oh, er, I'm a private investigator. My name's Murray Barber. I'm sorry to bother you but I'm looking into the disappearance of Melanie Foskett and I just wondered if I could ask Mr Cannon-Leigh about Adam. He had been one of the last people to see her."

"Oh. I thought Adam died years back? Well, I suppose if you give me your number I'll pass it on to my husband."

"Thank you very much. That would be a great help." Murray gave the number of his mobile and hung up the phone. What could he do now? The archives? Maybe there would be something on Melanie?

He searched back through the years until he found the summer of 1974.

"Bugger me! Forty-two pence a gallon of petrol!" He couldn't help but notice the adverts. Then he found the right edition, Friday 2nd August 1974.

Front page column asking if anyone had seen

Melanie? And a photograph... yes that was the same

young girl with her long blonde hair who had stood

in her underwear and dressed in cords and a

flowered blouse. Murray picked up his pen and

grabbed his notebook from his jacket pocket. He

needed to make a list of all the people he needed to

find and question. There was Mr Cannon-Leigh.

Melanie's mother, Catherine. Janet and/or her

father from the bookies and that other guy who

worked there. He'd have to try and find out who he

was, perhaps Janet would know? Murray paused as

it suddenly crossed his mind that seeing Janet again

could be quite a weird experience, having once been

her boyfriend? Then of course there was Danny

from the market. The only other person he could think of was Adam himself. How would he feel if Ali and Rita found him on the 'other side'? Strangely, he privately hoped that they didn't.

CHAPTER FOUR

By the time Jeff knocked on the door Murray had traced Catherine Foskett to a nursing home in Fowey on the south coast. He had called the reception and asked about paying the old lady a visit. Carly, the very helpful young lady on the other end of the phone line, had been quite enthusiastic as dear Mrs Foskett didn't receive many visitors since her husband had passed away a couple of years before. Murray did enquire as to the state of her mind to which he was informed straight up that she was as sharp as a chef's knife! Ten o'clock the following morning was booked for his visit.

Jeff arrived in shirt and trousers so Murray guessed he was on office time. He poured more coffee and the two friends settled down in the lounge.

"Ok Murray, I've got to admit this is your most way out case yet!"

"Yeah I know. I'm still finding it hard to get my head round it. Anyhow, what have you got?" Murray sat forward on the armchair, his own notebook at the ready.

"Right. July 1974. Melanie Foskett was due in at

work, Proctor Bookies owned and ran by Marcus Proctor, at 10am. She never turned up. She was reported missing the next day, Sunday, at twelve thirty lunchtime by her mother Catherine. Melanie never usually missed work and she wasn't seen at Freddie's party on the Saturday night either. Her Mum knew she was going but none of her friends saw her there."

"Melanie was going to the party too? I remember Janet asking me to pick her up…"

"Janet? Janet Proctor?" Jeff glanced across at Murray and sipped his coffee.

"Adam was seeing Janet but also seeing Melanie on the side."

"Oh…." Jeff paused and then studied Murray. "Did either know about the other?"

"Melanie knew about Janet. She was the daughter of her boss so we... they had to be a bit careful. Janet didn't know about Melanie as far as I could tell."

"Well... according to the report, the last people known to see her were Danny Williams who had a clothes stall on the market and, according to Danny, Adam Cannon-Leigh. Danny's statement is here but there's nothing from Adam... as I said, he died on the Saturday." Jeff cast another glance at his mate.

"Mmm, I'd like to find out how. Bothers me a bit. Un-nerving!" Murray ran his fingers through his hair and then sat up straight again. "So. What do we have? People to trace... I made a list, Catherine Foskett, Janet and her dad, Danny and there was another guy who worked in the bookies but I'm not sure who he was."

"Mmm, doesn't name anyone else. It's just a preliminary report. She was an adult and there weren't really any leads as such. She was seen alive that morning and I guess the assumption was that she just decided to take off somewhere."

"Not the impression I got from her..." Murray shrugged his shoulders in response to the look Jeff was giving him. "I know... I sound nuts! But seriously, she was chatting away and even told me to be careful what I said if I went in to place a bet!"

"Ok. It is an odd thing to just turn around and go somewhere. Disappear. Thing is, this case has never been closed but that doesn't mean she hasn't turned up. She may be alive and well, just no-one told the police."

"I hope she is. I'm going to see her mother tomorrow morning, ten o'clock. Found her in a nursing home in Fowey still with her marbles intact!"

"You've been busy!" Jeff closed the file and placed it on the coffee table. "Anything else I can do?"

"Err, have you got a list of contact details there by any chance?" he nodded at the file.

"Danny has a council house in Rame View Road. 1974 though Murray? The bookies is still there but it's a Ladbrokes now. I wouldn't hold out much hope. Does the mother still own a house? You never know, you might just find Melanie living in it?" Jeff finished his coffee and glanced at his watch. "Right, I'll leave you to it. You can keep this file, it's only a copy I ran off, but don't wave it around ok?"

"Brilliant!"

Murray saw Jeff out and although he wanted to sit and read the file properly, he still had bills to pay and a customer waiting. He grabbed his keys and laptop and headed out to his car.

CHAPTER FIVE

Mr Lee Woodley was a tall, 'expensive' looking man with greying temples. He was sat in his Mercedes in the carpark outside the private block that housed the rented flat of his mistress, Deborah. She worked in a florist, where Lee had met her while buying flowers for a woman he told her was his wife. Of course she hadn't been, she had been the previous mistress, but that was just the way he lived his life. Murray wasn't going to judge. He was only interested in the pay cheque at the end of the day. Mayflower Florist was where Deborah now was. The flat was empty and Lee was going to let Murray in so they could retrieve the cameras and discover what, if anything, she had been up to.

As Murray set to work dismantling his equipment and attaching it to his laptop so to view the film, Lee wandered around the flat in silence. Murray could hear him opening doors and drawers in the bedroom and wondered if she would notice when she came home, or whether in fact she would get the chance, she could find the locks changed by then?

"I'm ready." Murray finally called out when he had

the screen set. Lee wandered back into the lounge and stood with his hands clenched inside his pockets.

"Ok." he said without emotion. Murray selected fast-forward play and let the film roll. He wondered if Mr Woodley was always so good at hiding his feelings? Was he angry with Deborah because he thought she was cheating and taking advantage of his generosity? Or was he so hurt he was just shutting all his feelings off to protect himself?

They sped through the first day seeing no visitors, then a couple of girlfriends showed up before the twenty-something, very classically beautiful, Deborah was seen inviting a blonde-haired young man into the flat, pouring him a drink and getting very cosy on the settee. Murray wasn't sure whether or not to stop there. Lee was staring silently at the screen but made no effort to halt the proceedings. Murray let the film continue on. The young man stayed the night. Lee appeared on the screen the following day and after he left the young man returned. Lee's face still showed nothing. The third day was quiet, the forth Lee returned, and the fifth and then the young man was back. Finally Murray spoke up.

"Have you seen all you need to see? I can give you a copy of the whole thing if you need it?"

"Erm... yes, I'll take a copy." He seemed lost in thought for a few moments. Murray wondered if he was composing himself? "Actually.... I've seen that man somewhere before." Another thoughtful pause. "No, I can't place him." He turned his stare from the screen back towards Murray. "I'd like you to find out who he is for me. Can you do that?"

"Sure. Shouldn't take too long."

"Good. Do it. How long before I can have a copy?"

"I can do that now, only take a few minutes." Murray took a memory stick from inside his laptop bag and downloaded the film file. Ten minutes later both men had left the flat and returned to the carpark where they went their separate ways.

As Murray drove home he thought it was a pity he hadn't attached sound to the film but it was too late now. He'd have to ask Ali and Rita if they wouldn't mind listening out for a name. Maybe they could catch the guy on his next visit. Hopefully they would be getting back to him today sometime with news of Melanie? He parked up and headed for his front door, time for some more researching. As he entered his kitchen his mobile rang. It was Michelle, his own 'bit on the side'.

"Hi honey, just thought I'd check you're still alive. Haven't heard from you in a while."

"Yeah, I'm still here! Busy that's all, you know what my life's like now!"

"You got any exciting cases on then?" Michelle's voice always rose a tone or two when she spoke of his work, it thrilled her!

"I've just left a man who's mistress is cheating on him!" Murray chuckled at the irony.

"Oh dear. I would never do that to you."

"You wouldn't?" He was surprised.

"Mmm, no. Well not yet anyway. I quite like our relaxed arrangement. And I couldn't handle more than one man at a time. I don't know how you cope with your complicated life?" Right now Murray felt like he had two complicated lives but he could explain that to her when they next met up.

"Anyway, I called to see if you were free later? I've got the evening off and I couldn't think of anyone else I fancied spending it with!"

"Ah... I'm busy later...."

"Jenny?" She didn't sound angry, just a little disappointed.

"Sorry. Already arranged. When you off next?"

"Mmm, depends... Oh, the life of the other woman! Rained off for the girlfriend AGAIN!"

"I really don't mean to do this to you, it's just that I can be honest about cancelling with you. I can't tell Jenny I'm calling off a date with her so I can see my mistress!... I really am sorry."

"I suppose I forgive you, though most people would think I was totally out of my mind! Promise me you'll ring me soon."

"Promise, promise."

When the call was over a thought crossed Murray's mind. Maybe he could treat Michelle to a big bunch of flowers from the Mayflower Florist? Perhaps he could even be honest with Deborah and say they were for his 'other' girlfriend and see if he could get her talking about the young man on the film? It could be worth a try?

He made himself a corned-beef and mustard sandwich and sat down in front of his computer.

"Right." He took out his notebook. "Catherine we have. Next... Danny Williams, Daniel..." He typed the name into the search bar and waited. The man still lived in the same council house as in the report from 1974. Murray made a note of the telephone number and dialled.

There was only an answerphone so Murray decided to leave a message. He just stated his name and number and said he was calling regarding the disappearance of Melanie Foskett and could he please return his call. It did cross his mind whether or not Melanie actually was still missing but he felt too impatient to sit and do nothing for another day.

The next person on his list was Janet, or maybe he should check out the father? He decided to search Proctor Bookmakers instead. He knew it was silly but he felt nervous about meeting Janet... again. Proctor Bookmakers were now a limited company.

On-line betting. How things moved on! There was an e-mail address to 'contact us' through so that's what Murray did. He enquired as to whether Janet Proctor was available and a return request. It would probably be ignored he thought after he had sent it but then again, would it be a good idea to include too many details? His thoughts were interrupted...

"Boo!" It was Ali's most frequently used greeting!

"Ali?" Murray turned to face the middle of the room, unsure of exactly which corner the voice had sprung from.

"Afternoon Murray my man! It is afternoon isn't it?"

"Err, yes it is. Any news?" Murray held his breath.

"Yeah man." He didn't elaborate.

"Well?"

"Don't know if you really want to hear all this mate?" Ali was sounding more hesitant than Murray had ever heard him before.

"Ali, look... I'm in this now. I won't be able to put it down until I get all the answers..."

"Ok." Ali's voice moved over to the settee. "Melanie Foskett died in 1974. It seems something did happen to her when she went missing." Murray's heart sank. Now he really felt like he was on a mission.

"Have you found her?" he asked quietly.

"No... she's ... she's back down here somewhere." Silence fell over the room for what seemed like ages but was little more than a minute. "Afraid it doesn't help with what happened to her."

"No. Looks like I'll have to solve things the old-fashioned way." Murray didn't want to ask his next question but knew he had to. "What about Adam?" Again there was a pause.

"Same." Silence. "Doesn't necessarily mean what you might think man. Just means we can't find out much.. on our side, you know?"

"Yeah." Murray shook himself. "Doesn't mean anything, just have to do a bit more work myself, eh? Anyhow, I'll work on that but can you do me a favour...?"

"Sure man, what it is?"

"Is Rita here by the way?" Murray cocked his head as though to hear her breathing, which of course he knew he wouldn't!

"No. Her Mum's not good again. Not surprising at her age! But she likes to keep tabs on her."

"Oh. Is Rita ok?" Murray sounded worried.

"It's not nice to see someone you love die but for us, well, we're not losing them we're getting them back."

"Well, I hope she doesn't suffer. Tell Rita I'll be thinking of her won't you?"

"Yeah man. No worries. What did you want me to do?"

"Oh.. yeah. There's a woman called Deborah Skilling who I've just been filming, you know the case, Mr Lee Woodley?

"Oh yeah, the cheating mistress."

"That's the one. Well, yes she is cheating. This Lee reckons he's seen this young guy before but can't place him. You couldn't do a bit of bugging and find out a name for me could you? I can Google him then and find out the rest for myself."

"No worries. Anything else?" Murray gave it some thought but could think of nothing more so Ali left him to his thoughts. And a head full of thoughts he had.

CHAPTER SIX

Murray was still feeling somewhat distracted when he and Jenny headed out to the 'Spice Palace' to pick up their usual. Maybe Michelle would have made better company as he could have spoken openly about how he felt about the Melanie case to her. She knew about 'the voices' as Jeff put it. However, Jenny was more than sympathetic over his fall at Pam's, she was very good at the 'TLC' and at least he could explain his distraction as down to his head injury. She wasn't happy about him driving around working and had little time for such people as Lee Woodley. 'Serves him right! Cheating on his wife. Good to see someone like him get a taste of his own medicine!' Murray tried not to look as guilty as his client.

The curry went down well and so did the Merlot. Jenny wasn't sure at first if she should let Murray drink but he insisted anyway! After discussing her next business trip, planned for Paris the following week, they found themselves on the topic of Jeff and Kate's imminent arrival.

"... are you as worried as me about what we've agreed to get ourselves into?" she asked as she picked up her glass and snuggled alongside him on the settee.

"Godparents you mean? Don't even know exactly what we're expected to do. I should think the ceremony will be bad enough."

"Ooh, a good reason to shop for a new outfit! Hadn't thought about that."

"Will I have to wear a suit?"

"Definitely!" she pecked him on the lips. "You'll look fantastically sexy!"

"Mmm. So what do we have to do for this child anyhow?"

"I know I've got Godparents but to be honest I don't recall them 'doing' anything. Isn't it supposed to be giving spiritual guidance or something? Is that what they said? I'm not sure if Jeff and Kate have any religious views? Do they?"

Murray stared at the ceiling above them as he lay next to Jenny and thought about it.

"Ermm, I'm not sure. They don't go to church but that could be partly down to the life of a policeman." In his mind he did wonder, what with 'the voices', he had no idea what Jeff really thought?

The next morning, as Jenny headed out to work, Murray prepared himself for his trip to Fowey. He made sure he was clean-shaven and tidy. Catherine must have been in her forties when Melanie disappeared back in 1974 which would make her well into her seventies, if not her eighties, by now. She probably still didn't know what had happened to her daughter, in some ways, Murray wished he didn't either. He'd just have to be very careful what he said.

The harbour looked so picturesque as Murray drove down the hill into the seaside town. There was a huge ship being towed into the port up river which glided along behind it's tug looking out of scale with its surroundings. 'Majestic' was the word that sprung into Murray's mind. The sun was glaring but the temperatures were not that warm yet as he drove into the small private parking lot behind the home. It could easily be taken for one of the many hotels in the town but Murray double-checked the address and was satisfied he was at the right place.

Catherine was expecting him, in fact she had been ready and waiting in the conservatory since she finished her breakfast. Murray was led in and introduced to this tiny-framed, frail-looking woman who wore reading glasses and held a copy of Reader's Digest on her lap.

"Mr Barber, I assume?" she asked holding out her hand. Murray smiled and said 'hello' and took her hand before seating himself down and taking in the panoramic view of the river, less the ship of course which had now disappeared around the river's bend.

"It's so nice to have a visitor, especially such a mysterious one. Have we met before? I can't say I recall you."

"No, no we haven't. I'm a private investigator. I don't want to upset you, it's just that I came across the case of you're missing daughter, Melanie?"

"Oh." Catherine sounded quite calm and matter of fact but there was the evidence of long-burdened grief hiding behind the delicate frames of those reading glasses. "That was a long time ago. I think one has to accept that she met an un-timely end."

"Did anyone ever find out what happened?" Murray spoke as softly as he could.

"No." her voice was still calm as she gently shook her head. "There one minute, gone the next." She turned and smiled at him, though not with the eyes.

"Can you tell me about the other people who saw her just before... erm, well that last day?"

"Are you investigating it?" she asked sharply, studying him closely.

"I would like to. I think there needs to be an answer, some closure." she studied him some more before she answered him.

"Yes. That would be nice." she let out a sigh, a very life-long tired sigh. "I'm not sure what I can tell you after all this time that will be of any use? She had stayed with her gentleman friend the night before, I think that was the Friday...? Yes, the Friday night she stayed out. But she never missed work. She didn't particularly like her job but it paid ok. Her boss, Mr Proctor, he was always very short. Plain speaking if you like. the other man, what was his name...?" Murray hoped she would remember as he pulled out his notebook and pen. "..Harrison?... Jonathon Harrison. He was what you'd now call a bit of a chauvinist pig! Didn't like working with a woman, not unless she made a good cup of tea! Mel didn't like him very much. I don't think he held a very high opinion of her but she didn't deserve that from him. She was a good girl." Murray thought back to the sweet face of the blonde-haired girl he had woken up to and the snide remark the man in the bookies had made about who's car she had climbed out of. He took a distinct dislike to Mr Harrison. "I think he's dead now. Lung cancer I think it was. Always had a cigarette hanging from his mouth. Must be some ten years or so gone? And her boss too. He worked himself into an early grave. Heart-attack." She nodded as though to say 'there, told you so'. They may be dead, but that wouldn't stop Murray searching for them to get the answers he wanted.

"What about friends? Or maybe this gentleman friend?" Murray didn't meet her gaze.

"She was friendly with everyone. I know that morning she was supposed to have stopped and chatted to Danny. He had the clothes stall she liked. He had a bit of thing for her I think. But he was married." She shook her head dismissively. "There was the lad Jimmy who worked in the electrical store next to the bookmakers. He always went out of his way to say hello to her. Adam, that was the name of her friend. Only met him once. He seemed very nice too. But she didn't seem keen on making a big fuss about him." 'Probably because he was in a relationship already too' thought Murray. "You know, I really can't imagine anyone who knew her would have wanted to harm her Mr Barber. I think it must have been someone else. Some stranger who managed to whisk her away. Perhaps asking for help? Directions maybe? It was a busy market. Saturday morning, ten o'clock. No-one noticed anything out of the ordinary, no woman screaming for help or anything. I know, I spent weeks of Saturdays on that market afterwards asking anyone and everyone." The grief in the eyes was starting to show more. She blinked hard, forcing back any sign of tears.

Murray didn't want to upset the old lady anymore. He had a name to put to the work colleague. He gave her his card and promised to let her know as soon as he found anything out. She seemed only too grateful that someone, though she didn't know him, was prepared to take the time to help her daughter, even if she already accepted the fact that it was way too late.

CHAPTER SEVEN

Murray could have rushed straight home and logged back into his computer but he didn't. The town had an enchanting quality and the sun was getting warmer. He decided to take a stroll down to the quay where he bought himself a freshly made Cornish pasty, sat himself down on the wall and watched the orange-painted ferry boat chug its way back and forth across the river to the village on the other side. He just wanted to take half an hour to himself. Not to think of anything in particular, not the case or any of its mind-bending possibilities, just to sit and appreciate being alive.

Finally, he set off for home but decided on a detour on the way. Mayflower Florist was a modern establishment, it looked clean and tidy with a tv screen on the wall showing adverts for different arrangements and explaining delivery and care of plants, etc. Murray stood fascinated until the assistant spoke in his ear.

"Can I be of any assistance sir?" Murray turned and instantly recognized Deborah the 'mistress'.

"Oh, sorry! I was well away there! I er, I'm after a nice bunch of 'sorry' flowers." he smiled.

"Oh dear!" she laughed. It was a laugh that would have put any condemned man at ease, she must have done this before. "Well now, is this a 'serious sorry' or 'just another sorry'?"

"It's an on-going type of sorry. Err.. I'm not sure I

should admit to what I've been up to."

"Oh dear again!" What she said was very flirtatious but how she said it was pure classy charm! "A serial offender?" she pulled a quizzical frown at him and then once again burst into a smile.

"It's the girlfriend." Murray whispered his admission. "The er.. other girlfriend, if you catch my drift?"

"I think you mean 'the mistress'." she winked in a conspiratorial manner. "Ok." The tone was back to saleslady. "Do you know which flower is her favourite?"

"Not really." Murray stared around at the mass of colour and variety. "I've never bought her flowers before but I keep putting her off because the regular lady..." He stopped and looked a little embarrassed.

"...Well, you know, first lady comes first, the 'other one' knows the score?"

"Only too well I'm afraid." She glanced about her for a choice of bloom. "How about chrysanthemums? They're pretty safe." She held her hand towards a display.

"Sure. They look lovely. Do you deliver?"

"Can do. Where to?"

"Restaurant just out of town, The Hayloft?"

"Oh yes, I know it. We can do that certainly. Let me take some details." She moved to the desk and took the order and delivery details along with a payment that made Murray think twice before calling in on a florist again. Next time the supermarket would be quite sufficient! As his card payment went through he took one last chance at getting her to talk.

"I can't believe someone would treat you as second best, you come over as a very put together young lady?"

"Thank you." She glanced up at him. "It takes all sorts I suppose!" She wasn't going to elaborate. Murray might as well give up and head home.

Back at his flat once more, Murray set himself up at his computer with the usual coffee and notebook beside him. Glancing down his list of names he decided to try Jonathon Harrison on the death register, just in case Catherine had been wrong. He didn't want to waste Ali and Rita's time, if 'time' was the right word? While he waited he checked his e-mails and was surprised to see a response from

Proctor Bookmakers. He clicked on it and found a short message saying that Miss Janet Proctor didn't reply to personal messages but she could be reached through another e-mail address. The address was attached so Murray made a note of it and switched screens back to his search. Jonathon Harrison had indeed died over a decade ago just as Catherine had said. He thought he might as well check Marcus Proctor while he was at it just so he was prepared if he got to speak to Janet. Again the result was as Catherine had said. Marcus Proctor too had died some years before.

"Hello Murray!"

Murray sat up and spun around.

"Rita?"

"Yes, it's me. What's happening?" She sounded

nonchalant, or maybe tired... if that was possible.

"Just researching some names from 1974. I thought you'd be with Ali?"

"We're not joined at the hip you know Murray!" That brightened her tone.

"I know, I didn't mean that. How's your mum by the way, Ali said she's not been too good?" Murray clasped his hands between his knees and looked sympathetically towards the kitchen door where Rita's voice was coming from.

"She's ok. Still hanging in there. Very resilient my mother! Is there anything I can do while I'm here or should I go and find Ali?"

"You sound like you're trying to avoid him. You two haven't had an argument or anything like that have you?" Murray was genuinely concerned. Rita started laughing.

"Me and Ali! Are you serious? You are aren't you? Oh Murray, no, no we haven't! But we do spend time apart sometimes."

"Well, that's ok then, as long as nothing's wrong. I can't imagine one of you without the other." Rita was still laughing.

"So." She said. "Can I do anything?"

"Er, yes actually. I've got two deceased persons here from 1974. There's Janet Proctor's dad, Marcus. He owned the Bookies where Melanie worked and Jonathon Harrison who was her co-worker. They may not have anything to add but I think it's worth asking anyhow. Do you think you could track them down?"

"We can give it a try. Ali has headed off in search

of this mistress you asked him about but we can do both between us."

"DON'T let this interfere with your mother Rita." Murray emphasized where her priority lay.

"I won't, don't you go worrying! Marcus Proctor and Jonathon Harrison, ok got it. Get back to you later." And so she was gone.

CHAPTER EIGHT

Murray's evening was interrupted by a call from his mother who had been talking to her sister, his aunt Pam, who had also phoned to check up on him. And a text from Jenny who was up to her neck in preliminaries and other 'stuff' in preparation for the up-coming trip across the Channel. Finally after he managed to soak in a relaxing bath, he received a call from Michelle.

"... you should have seen my face! I wish I had seen my face! That really was so sweet of you. I don't expect it every time you dump me for her... no actually, I take that back, you can buy me flowers every time you call off or put off a date, right?"

"Ok. Flowers once a week then. What day do you prefer for these deliveries?"

"Haha! Very funny. Anyway, how's your day been? Or do I sound too much like the little woman at home when I ask that?"

"I'll tell you if you're really interested? I can talk about it easier with you than I can with Jen."

"Really? Oh go on then, tell me, tell me!" She was

teasing on the other end of the line, but Murray had experienced quite a profound day.

"Seriously, I've had quite a couple of days. I had a fall at my Aunt's the other day and knocked myself out..."

"You what? You didn't say!"

"I'm ok, honest. It's just when I was out cold I had this weird dream set back in 1974. Only now I've found out that the people in my dream were real and what I dreamt happen did actually happen. It's so far out..."

"Wow! What happened in your dream?... Hang on... can I come over?"

"Now? It's pretty late?"

"You wouldn't want me to stay then?" She sounded a little put out. "I could have thanked you properly for the flowers but hey, if ...."

"Sure. Come over. I mean it. It'd be much easier to talk over a glass of wine anyhow...."

Michelle had arrived forty minutes later. Still in her crisp white work blouse but smelling of something flowery rather than a restaurant kitchen. Murray had his notebook out on the coffee table next to two freshly poured glasses of Tempranillo. Just the table lamps were on. They sat and drank their way through the first glass while Murray filled her in on the peculiar goings on and how he wasn't sure if any of it was just in his mind? Yet the proof he had accumulated since could only mean one thing, that he 'dreamt' part of a past memory, possibly from his last life.

"And how does that make you feel?" She asked him

with a look of confusion on her face.

"I really don't know. Like I say, I just can't quite accept it. But putting that aside, I want to find out what happened to Melanie and who did it to her. And maybe what happened to Adam as well although I'm not sure that I'll feel any better if I do find out."

"Knowing how you died? Mmm. Not sure I'd sleep easy if I knew something like that."

"I think I'm going to concentrate on Melanie. Her mother's really sweet and I feel now that I've sort of made a promise to her to conclude this. Give her some answers before she finds them out for herself on the other side." Michelle was sitting back up straight and placing her glass down on the table as he spoke. "What's the matter?" he asked.

"I was just thinking, it's still an open case, there might be a murderer out there somewhere? You say Ali and Rita never get their facts wrong, she did die. Then again, she's still not been found... is she an unclaimed Jane Doe or is she still lying out there somewhere, undiscovered?" It was a chilling thought. Murray sat up straight next to her, he felt more determined than ever to get to the bottom of this whole business.

Murray got up early the next morning and headed to the kitchen to make coffee. He had intended on treating Michelle to breakfast in bed but he was disturbed by the ever so familiar sound of Ali making him jump.

"Boo!"

"Morning Ali. I'm not quite awake enough yet. On your own?" Murray was watching the kettle boil.

"No. You have guests in the lounge! When you're ready mate." Ali's voice moved away through the kitchen door.

"Who's here?... Ali?" He left the kettle where it was and walked quietly into the lounge, glancing around the empty looking room as he entered.

"Morning Murray, this is Jonathon Harrison. He worked alongside Melanie at Proctor Bookies." Rita spoke in barely more than a whisper as though she was worried about waking Murray's companion. She was sat on the armchair.

"Morning Rita. Hello Mr Harrison?" Murray let his eyes sweep the room awaiting a reply to help him home in on the position of his new guest.

"Mr Barber." A voice acknowledged. It came from the right-hand end of the settee so that was where Murray would aim his questions.

"Hello. Sorry to bother you like this. I take it these two have told you I'm investigating Melanie's disappearance. You know she's never been found?"

"So it seems. I hope you don't think I had anything to do with it?" The man spoke sharply, almost defensively.

"Well now you're here I think we can cross you off the list. She died back in 1974 according to whoever informs you lot of these things, no disrespect but please don't try and explain 'up there', I'd rather not know too much until I need to." Murray was still tired but made an attempt to shake himself. He should have poured that coffee out. "How much do you remember about that day back in '74?"

"Not much." Harrison sniffed. "She was just a kid, not a bad lass, no trouble. She'd turn up for work, keep the punters happy, flutter her eyelashes like they do. She was never lippy or back-talking. Nice girl when all said and done." He seemed to be relaxing a little more now.

"She was due in at work for ten that day, right?" Murray had picked up his notebook from the coffee table and sat himself down at his desk.

"She was never late. No sign of her that day though."

"I thought you had seen her get out of Adam's car?" Murray was recalling his dream.

"Oh... yeah I did. Forgot that! He was seeing Janet, the boss's daughter. That's where the money lay anyhow. Still, I could see the attraction of Melanie, she was a pretty young thing." Murray felt his back stiffen. He hadn't considered Adam as a gold-digger. Harrison went on. "I guess he must have spent the night with Mel. She jumped out of his car on the far side of the market, she stopped and said something to him and then I guess she must have cut across the square to work. I was already on the right side of the market for work. I turned and headed into the shop when she was still yacking. Maybe she stayed with him...? Then again, she couldn't have, he came in. He dropped off a dress for Janet about half-ten. Boss was still shouting about where was she. I suppose..." Now he sounded thoughtful. "... he could have done something with her during that time? Maybe he got her back in the car and knocked her out somehow. Parked up and then acted all normal-like? Could be possible?"

"I don't think so." Murray felt that was spoken a little too dismissively. "Well, probably not. Anyhow, thankyou Mr Harrison. Is there anything else you remember before you go? Anything happen in the days before?" There was a short pause.

"Nothing out of the ordinary that I can recall. I was a lot older than her. Yes, we all had a drink in the 'Stag' after work sometimes but I didn't know about her private business, not more than I saw with my own eyes. We just worked together."

"Ok, no problem. Thanks again for your help."

Murray looked at the empty page in his notebook. Jonathon Harrison hadn't told him anything he didn't already know. He put the book down, got up and returned to the kitchen where he re-boiled the kettle. What was he's next step? He must write an e-mail to Janet for one. Try Danny Williams again?

His thoughts were broken by a warm arm gently wrapping itself around his waist. He hadn't even heard Michelle get up.

"You were talking to someone?" She spoke quietly.

"Mmm. Only Ali and Rita with that Jonathon guy from the bookies. Couldn't tell me anything though. You sleep alright?"

"Yeah. Shall I cook breakfast?" She kissed the back of his shoulder.

"We'll cook it together and then I must get back to this case."

"Have you always been a private investigator? I mean, how did you get into it in the first place?" She moved to the fridge and took out some eggs.

"No. I thought about being a postie like my dad when I was a kid. But those early mornings, especially in all weathers, put me off as I got older. I worked as a porter up at the old hospital when I went to college. For a while anyway, quit pretty quickly, used to freak me out a bit. Too many voices even for me! Finished my year at college and started working in a music and video store."

"What did you study at college?"

"Business studies and basic accounting. Boring I know!" He smiled at her over his shoulder as he took two plates from the cupboard.

"Bloody useful though. Especially as you work for yourself. But how did the sleuthing start?"

"Jeff, actually!" They dished up the eggs on toast

and took their coffees into the lounge. "He was dating this girl Caroline... Caroline Pointer, and he was convinced she was cheating on him, so, being his best mate I said I'd find out for him. I followed her and she WAS cheating! I just enjoyed the freedom of the work. Thing is, the more jobs you do, the more you realize just how boring it all becomes!"

"You're still doing it?"

"Yeah, but I don't think I could hack working for someone else now. If I had to, I would. If the work dried up. Got to pay the bills!"

"Aren't you working this case for free? Or are you going to charge yourself!"

"Haha! Honestly, I've never had a case quite like this one. I'm doing this for me... and I'm doing it for

Melanie....."

CHAPTER NINE

'For the attention of Miss Janet Proctor

My name is Murray Barber. I'm a private

investigator looking into the disappearance of

Melanie Foskett on 27th July 1974. Her

whereabouts have never been discovered. I would

very much like to ask you about this incident. If you

could please reply I would be grateful.'

He sent the e-mail and hoped for the best. The

next thing he did was redial Danny Williams'

number but, yet again, it went to answerphone. He

left another message. Maybe he still worked on the

market? It was worth a try. He shut down his computer, picked up his keys and headed out the door.

The market square was 'bustling' as they say. It still looked pretty much the same as Murray had dreamt it. Some of the stalls had changed, or at least, their goods had. The sun was up and people were smiling and chatting away. Murray wandered up and down the rows looking for a clothes stall and hopefully a stallholder who looked similar, if not a lot older, than Danny Williams.

At one end of the square Murray stopped and glanced up the side street. Yes, there was the bookmakers, a branch of a large group now. He wondered whether the Proctor family still had any connections with the business? It was unlikely. He turned and studied the layout of the stalls. Could he remember exactly where Danny's plot had been? It was pretty likely he'd still be in the same place. Murray smiled to himself as he watched a grey haired, weather-beaten man give the same sale chat as he had heard once before. He strolled over to the stall and waited, like he had also done once before, for the man to finish his sale.

"Danny Williams?" he asked.

"Who's asking?" Danny looked him up and down.

"I tried to call you. My name is Murray Barber, I'm a..."

"Private investigator. Yeah, I got your message." He didn't take his eyes from Murray. "What did you want?"

"I'm looking into the disappearance of Melanie

Foskett...."

"Why? That happened years ago. Poor girl was never seen again but I doubt there's anything that can be got from it now."

"Do you remember what happened that day? Would you mind just running through it for me quickly?" The man glanced around him. He greeted another customer and pointed out a new line that he had just had in. He then turned back to Murray.

"She said hello to me on her way across the square. She always did. She said hello to a lot of people. I was busy, I didn't look at where she went after she past me."

"Ok." Murray could tell the man didn't want to discuss it. He tried one last question. "Who else had a stall here back then? Is there anyone else here I could ask? There's an old lady in a home who would really like some answers about what happened to her daughter." That got the desired effect. Danny stopped and studied Murray again, perhaps it was a look of regret on his face? He nodded over towards a fruit and veg stall along the row.

"Ask Kenny. He was here that morning and she always bought an apple from him for her lunch." Murray thanked Danny and wandered along to Kenny's stall.

He too was busy grinning and chatting away in a friendly manner to everyone. Murray waited his turn, glancing back to see that Danny was standing watching his every move. He then introduced himself to Kenny who came out to the side of the stall.

"A private investigator eh? Didn't realize there were any real ones of them about! Old Mrs Foskett's still around is she? She was a nice girl, came down every Saturday at the end of the day and bought up what she needed cheap! Good customer! Melanie was a lovely girl, can't imagine anyone who knew her wanting to do her any harm."

"Danny just said she always bought an apple for her lunch?"

"Yeah, yeah she did. Granny smith, as green and sharp as she could get! She did that day too. Think Jimmy stopped her to chat. He was smitten with her. Just out of school, sixteen? Seventeen maybe?"

"Jimmy?" Murray pulled his notebook from his pocket.

"Jimmy Beckinsworth. Funny lad, quiet and odd!

Liked to straighten things. You'd see him working his way around the shop, he worked in the electrical store that used to be next to the bookies, straighten all the stock up! He used to do the same as he walked through the market sometimes. Some didn't like it but he was harmless, just couldn't help himself!"

"Jimmy Beckinsworth." Murray repeated as he wrote the name down. Someone else to trace. "Thanks, you've been a lot more helpful than Danny. I don't think he was keen to speak to me."

"Well, I suppose that's understandable. It was a bad day for him, lost one of his mates that day and then, of course, the police suspected the guy might have been involved..."

"Adam?" Murray shot a shocked glare at Kenny.

"Yeah. If they had known him they probably wouldn't have looked at him but there was a rumour going round that he might have had something to do with it."

"Really?" Murray felt the market spin a little. His mind flashed back to his dream. Surely he hadn't been involved? He couldn't have been, he would have remembered?

"He was a bit of a wide boy. Liked the girls even though he was dating the girl from the bookies, the daughter that is. But he was harmless."

Murray thanked the man and made his way back to his car. His head was still swimming as he sat and tried to remember his dream clearly. Surely he hadn't had time to harm Melanie in any way. She had left him at his car and walked off into the market. He had then sat inside the cafe until Janet had met him and then he had stopped at Danny's stall, picked up the dress and gone straight to the bookies where Melanie had already gone missing. No, it couldn't have been him. Besides, he would have been one of those 'go straight to hell' lot that Ali and Rita had referred to before. It was nice to think that there was still someone out there who wanted to protect his memory, Danny, but Adam was being crossed off the suspect list.

He headed back home. As he walked in he switched on his computer, he might as well run a search on this Jimmy lad. He didn't get that far however, as there was a reply to the e-mail he sent Janet. He opened it to find it held a single phone number. He sat straight down and dialled. It was answered immediately.

"Hello?"

"Hello, can I speak to Janet Proctor please?" Murray wasn't sure if this was a direct line but he kept his fingers crossed.

"Speaking. Is that Murray Barber?"

"Yes. Thank you for getting back to me so quickly and directly..." He felt strange talking to his 'one-time girlfriend'.

"No problem. I remember Melanie well. You know she worked for my dad?"

"Yes. I've just come back from the market. I've just spoken to a couple of the stall holders."

"Oh, nice." She sounded a little cold, hiding her emotions maybe? Murray couldn't tell without seeing her face. "What did you want from me anyway?"

"Could I ask you about what you remember about that day?" There was a silence on the other end of the phone. Murray waited...

"Do you know Estover?"

"Er, yes?"

"I'll give you my address, can you come over?"

"That would be great." He was hesitant but he couldn't let his twisted emotions about his possible past get in the way of finding Melanie. He took down the address in Estover and ended the call. He picked up his notebook and keys and grabbed his jacket. He didn't make it out of the door however, Ali's voice rang out from the kitchen doorway.

"Murray my man where you going?"

"Out! You got some news for me?" He paused in

front of his front door.

"Yeah, brought you another visitor. Aren't we on good form today?"

"Er, yeah you are!" It was only hours since Jonathon Harrison had left. "Is this Marcus Proctor?"

"Yeah man. You coming back in?" Murray put down his keys and took off his jacket. Sitting himself back down at his desk, he pulled his notebook back out at the ready.

"Hello Mr Proctor?"

"Good afternoon." Murray recognized the rough sounding tones from the bookmakers during his dream.

"I was just about to go and visit your daughter, Janet?"

"Really? You go gentle with her. She went through a lot over this business."

"I will, don't worry. I don't suppose there's a lot you can add but do you remember that Saturday morning?"

"I've been thinking about it. Yes, I do recall some of it. The girl didn't turn up for work. Not like her at all. Sent Janet's lad out to look for her but seems no-one knew where she'd gone. Her mother came in at the end of the afternoon as people had been asking her where Melanie was. She got very upset very quickly. I told her the girl had probably gone off shopping for the day most likely. Maybe she just ran away? Apparently that wasn't the case." The man paused before he continued. "Later on that evening she never attended a party that she was expected at. Lot of fuss... upsetting night.... what with what happened. Still, no, I don't think I can help with young Melanie. She's moved on now according to this young man." He was referring to Ali.

"Yeah man, we can't get hold of her. But we do know her date of death, it was that Saturday."

"Oh well, thank you for coming so quickly Mr Proctor. I won't keep you, or your daughter. She's expecting me now so I'd better make a move."

CHAPTER TEN

Janet Proctor lived in an average, modern looking semi-detached house. There was a year old BMW sitting on the drive so she wasn't doing too badly for herself. She had put on weight since his vision of her from 1974 and her hair, although obviously dyed, was neatly tied back in a long ponytail. She welcomed Murray in and offered him a drink. It was much too early for him to accept anything alcoholic so she made him a coffee instead.

As Murray sat sipping his coffee and resting his notebook on his knee, he thought how little there was left of the 'young Janet'. She seemed very matter-of-fact and there wasn't any of the 'daddy dearest' type talking. Something had hardened her up. She was single? A surprise from what Murray could remember of her but then maybe that was down to being part of the gambling world?

"So you want to know about Melanie? What

exactly do you want me to tell you?" Was there a touch of dislike in her tone? Murray wondered if she had known, or maybe found out later, about him... Adam, and Melanie?

"Do you remember that Saturday when she went missing?"

"Vaguely.... I had to go and get a present for my mother from my dad. He usually sent me out. I caught up with my then boyfriend, Adam Cannon-Leigh, on the way into the shop and got him to pick me up a dress for a party...." She stopped short, took a puff on her cigarette, blowing out the smoke above her head, and then continued. "He picked me up a dress for a party we were going to that night. When I got into the shop Dad was already shouting about her being late. He sent me straight out again though so I don't know what went on after that. She wasn't at Freddie's party, I know that much."

"It wasn't a very good party I suppose, what with people wondering what had happened to her?"

"You could say that." She spoke without looking at him. She took a sip of her coke and whatever it was and stared up at her computer screen which stood on a dining table to the side of them. "Sorry, got to keep an eye on business."

"You're not in the betting game anymore then?" Murray asked.

"Yeah, but sold up the shops about five years back. Make better money on-line now. Hardly any staff and next to no over-heads. Racing, sport, games and even bingo. Keeps me busy." She said it like an excuse. It did make him wonder why she had become so cold. Should he ask her about Adam? She had already mentioned him.

"You mentioned your boyfriend, Adam? I found out he had died. On that same day apparently, he had nothing to do with her death I suppose?" She looked at him for a moment. It wasn't a glare but something else, more gentle. Murray couldn't quite read it.

"You ask that because he was seeing her I take it?"

"I had heard he was." He spoke gently, remembering what her father had just told him. "Did you know?"

"Not that morning. I found out later... at Freddie's." She was studying him again. Murray wondered whether any of these people could see any of Adam in him? "Do you have any idea what happened to her then?" It was a sharp change of subject.

"Not yet. She was never seen again, not to this day. It's most likely she died that day. Her mother has hired me." He lied.

"I didn't know her mother. I don't even know how long she and Adam had been seeing each other. I suppose we're better off not knowing some things."

"I'm sorry you got hurt." Had he said that out loud?

"You've nothing to be sorry for. Life's a bastard and then you die." She put her cigarette out and then placed another one between her lips ready to light.

"Erm.. Adam died that same day..." He might as well ask, it might be important. "...was he still alive for the party?"

"He went to the party, yes. Took me..." She stopped short again.

"I'm sorry if this is painful?"

"Stop apologizing Mr Barber... If you knew how he died then you'd understand me maybe." At this point the phone rang and Janet got to her feet and opened the door, a hint for him to leave. He did so with a nod of thanks as she lit the cigarette in her mouth and turned to answer her phone.

Murray sat back in his car. Once again his mind was in a whirl. This case was so close to home that he was feeling sick at the possibilities of what he might find out. How had Adam died? It was becoming clear that he was going to have to find out.

Back at home once more, he was greeted by the warm smile of Jenny and her freshly dyed blonde hair with honey high-lights.

"Do you like it?" she beamed as she spun around for him to get the full show.

"Lovely! This in aid of Paris next week?" He snapped out of his deep thoughts, life was still moving on.

"This is in aid of ME! I was getting bored." No surprise there! "How are you now? Head better?"

"A bit. Work keeps its cogs turning."

"Anything exciting on?" She had bought some shopping over with her and reaching the kitchen, she cut him a piece of chocolate cake. "Here, I treated us." They sat at the table. Should he tell her about Adam? She wouldn't believe any tale about reincarnation. He decided to start with Woodley.

"That guy who suspected his mistress of cheating on him was right."

"Serves him right! He's doing the same to his wife."

"Mmm." Murray tried hard to keep the guilt from his expression. "He wants me to find out about this guy she's seeing now though."

"Not going to do anything silly to him is he?" She paused mid-mouthful and stared at Murray.

"Hope not? Hadn't really thought about it."

"Murray! Just be careful. You should think about these things you know."

"Yeah, maybe. My mind was on my other case."

"What other case is that?"

"An old lady wants to find out what happened to

her missing daughter. She disappeared in 1974."

"Wow!" Jenny stared at him again. "That's a long time ago. Do you think she ran off or did something happen to her?"

"I would say she's dead." He knew that for sure but wasn't going to attempt explaining everything to Jenny.

"I've been interviewing a few people from that time but no real clues yet. She seemed a nice girl with a lot of friends. No reason for anyone to hurt her."

"What's the official standing?"

"Jeff brought me over the file. It's still an open 'missing person' case. Left on the shelf now however. Doesn't help much either."

"Do you think you'll be able to solve it babe?" She

stood and stepped towards the kitchen with her empty plate.

"Hope so."

"Coffee?" she asked. Murray nodded. "Maybe it was random? Grabbed off the street or something?"

"She was in a market square. On her way to work on a Saturday morning."

"Oh, well someone would have seen any funny business then. If she didn't run off by herself she must have gone with someone she knew." Murray sat silently. He was praying that it wasn't Adam. "How many people are on your list?" She returned to the table with the coffees.

"Oh thanks love. Err... the boyfriend, the work colleagues, couple of stall holders. Oh, and a lad from the shop next door. I meant to look him up."

He got up and switched on his computer. He opened his notebook and typed the name James Beckinsworth in the search bar. They waited but no address came up on the screen. "Might as well try the death register then." Murray shrugged.

"Oh nice!" Jenny stroked Murray's head gently, he flinched. "You are still hurt. Maybe you should go back to the doc's with that?"

"No need. I'm fine if you don't touch it!" He pecked her on the forehead and then glanced back at the screen as a result came up. 'No result.' "Well he's not dead then." Murray frowned at the screen. "I suppose he could be abroad?"

"So what now?"

"Dunno. How about I take the rest of the day off. We catch an early film, the pub, a takeaway and an early night?"

"Sound's very romantic. Who needs Paris!" she kissed him tenderly on the lips....

CHAPTER ELEVEN

Murray woke the next morning to the sound of a flute playing. It was coming from the bathroom. He got up quietly, trying not to disturb Jenny and followed the music.

"Morning Ali?" he whispered as he shut the bathroom door behind him.

"Morning Murray mate. How do you like my gentle 'hello I'm here'?"

"Very nice! Much better than the usual loud

shout!"

"Got some news on your mistress' new lover."

"Who?" Murray took a moment to shake himself awake. "Oh, Woodley's case?"

"Yeah man. He stayed till the early hours and then we followed him home. Got an address and a name for you. Got the name from his post."

"Brilliant! Rita with you or ...is everything ok with her mum?"

"She was with me but she's shot off now. Her old lady's not ready to give in just yet!"

"Ah right. As long as Rita's ok. What's this name and address then?"

The two of them crept into the lounge where Murray found his notebook amongst the discarded plates, take-away dishes and glasses.

"About time you got a new one of them, Murray mate!"

"Yeah, have to finish the cases in it first though." he smiled at his tatty notebook. "Right let's just run a check on this guy, what's his name?"

"Andy Spires...14 Castle Street..."

Murray entered the details into his computer and waited.

"Who is this guy, do you know?"

"A married man!"

"Really?" Murray turned to stare at the space next to his right shoulder. "Oh dear. A lot of people in this line waiting to get hurt it would seem."

"Murky waters Murray my man."

The search didn't bring anything new up. The man had both a facebook page and a twitter account but didn't do much on either. It did state on the first that he worked as a wedding planner. Murray made his notes and sat back.

"Thanks Ali. Job done. I'll call Mr Woodley in a bit and give him this." He glanced over towards the bedroom door. There came the sound of Jenny stirring. He got up and made his way quietly to the kitchen and put the kettle on. Ali followed him.

"Anything else man?"

"Well. You can't tell me who killed Melanie can you? Apparently Adam was suspected." He spoke in a quiet whisper.

"Nah man. She could tell me if she was around or I could find out if she had done something as bad herself. But I shouldn't worry, it can't be you, you wouldn't be here if you had killed her."

"I was hoping that. So what happened to her Ali? I'm hitting a brick wall. And dare I ask how Adam died? Janet said something yesterday but, to be honest, I'm scared what I might find out."

"It's a bit tricky Murray. Doors tend to close if things shouldn't be said. Have you looked to see if he had any close family? They could probably tell you what you want to know... Or don't want to know!"

"I'd forgotten about his family. I'll do that..."

"Murray? Babe, you up?" Jenny's sleepy, or maybe hung over, voiced croaked from the bedroom.

With breakfast over, Jenny headed off to the office and left Murray to clear up. He chucked the rubbish in the bin and soaked the glasses and dishes in the sink. He then returned to his desk and redialled the number he had written down for Mr J. Cannon-Leigh. This time a man's voice answered.

"Hello?"

"Oh, hello. Is that Mr Cannon-Leigh?"

"Yes, this is John. Who's this?"

"Hello, my name is Murray Barber. I'm a private investigator. I did leave a message with your wife the other day, I'm sorry to keep bothering you, it's just that I've been hired by the mother of Melanie Foskett to look into the circumstances of her disappearance back in 1974. She's never been found."

"Oh, right. I'm sorry, I never got your message." He sounded curt, emphasizing the part where he hadn't received the message. Maybe things weren't too good between him and his wife? "How can I help?"

"Er, could you tell me how you are related to Adam Cannon-Leigh?"

"We're cousins. Dads are brothers. We hung out a lot before... well, before he died."

"I'm very sorry about that. I understand it was accidental?" Murray held his breath waiting to hear what the man was going to say next.

"If you can call being pushed down a staircase accidental, then yes it was an accident!"

"Is that what happened?" Murray heard the words but wasn't sure if they were coming from his own mouth. He would never be able to put into words just how he was feeling at that moment.

"Mmm. That spoilt girlfriend of his. Janet? She'd

found out he was seeing this Melanie at the same time as dating her. Why she was so surprised I'll never know, he was known to be popular with the ladies."

"Oh..." Murray was struggling with words. He had to pull himself together and find out what he needed to know. He took a deep breath and stared at his notebook. "Were you at this party?"

"Yeah. Most people were. Freddy held great parties!" It sounded like the man was reminiscing. Murray could picture a smile spreading across John Cannon-Leigh's face. "Except for that party of course. Gossip was already flying round about Melanie disappearing. Adam unfortunately drank too much and then things started slipping out. Janet went mad and they had one hell of a row.

People tried to separate them. Someone took Adam upstairs and someone else took Janet outside but she wouldn't stay there. She ran back up and started shouting at him again and then she started pushing him. He was very drunk. They said he lost his footing and slipped but... well, if she pushed him.. he wouldn't have slipped if she hadn't pushed him." Murray was quiet. He was thinking about Janet. The cold, hard looking woman she had become. She had said if he knew how Adam had died, he'd understand. Yes, understand why she became the person she did. Regret? Guilt? Both hard to live with. "Mr Barber? Are you still there?"

"Sorry." Murray snapped himself back into focus. "I'm just making some notes. Err... Did you hear anything said at the party that could help me?

Anyone suggest who might have taken Melanie?"

"Well, lots was said. I think the general consensus was that Jimmy probably saw what happened. He was a bit odd. Used to watch people, including Melanie."

"Ah, yes I think his name has come up before..." Murray knew it had and now he under-lined it. He could ask Jeff to run a check on the guy, he might have more luck? "Well, thank you Mr Cannon-Leigh. You've been very helpful. Again, I'm sorry to have bothered you."

"No problem. I'm sorry I didn't return your call. If you do find out what happened to her, please let me know. It may sound silly, but.. well I'd like to be able to go down my cousin's grave and tell him too."

Murray went cold....

CHAPTER TWELVE

Murray sat and stared at his notebook for quite a while after the phone call had ended. Eventually he got up and finished the washing up. He then pulled himself together and called Mr Woodley. He passed on the information and asked what he planned to do with it? Nothing. He just wanted to know. And now he also knew where he knew Mr Spires from, he had been his wedding planner. Providing what had been a wonderful day for himself and Mrs Woodley. Strange how small the world was? He and Deborah must have met in the florist, a wedding planner would have to have a good relationship with a florist! Satisfied that he no longer cared what Mr Woodley was going to do about his situation, Murray told him he would send the bill and ended the call. He then dialled Jeff's number.

"Jeff? Not at the hospital yet then mate?" Murray joked.

"Not yet. I'm starting to get impatient now! How are you doing?"

"Not too bad. Head's better. I'm stuck on this old case."

"Was it you? This Adam guy?"

"I think so. No-one's saying for sure but... who knows? Anyhow, Melanie Foskett. The last person to see her in the market was probably a young lad by the name of Jimmy Beckinsworth. He worked in the electrical shop next to the bookies. He was a bit weird, OCD or something by the sound of it. Anyway, I can't track him down, you couldn't try and find him for me could you? I can't find a death certificate for him."

"Hang on, Jimmy Beckinsworth. How old was he?" Jeff was making notes.

"Just out of school. Seventeen give or take a year?"

"So seventy-four..... I make that a late fifties birth then?"

"Somewhere around there."

"I'll have a look and get back to you ok, don't like to keep the line busy!"

"Ok, cheers mate!"

What was Murray going to do while he waited? He had cleared his back jobs before he went over to help his aunt. He decided there was no time like the present to write up Woodley's bill and update his books. He made himself another cup of coffee, it crossed his mind that maybe he drank too much coffee, and set to work.

He finished his paperwork and sat back with his notebook open in front of him. Would he ever get his head around the whole idea of living a previous life? Probably not! So, who could have had time to whisk Melanie off into oblivion? He was sure it wasn't Adam. He knew exactly what Adam had done between dropping Melanie off and finding out she had gone missing. Who was next? Danny? Could he have left the stall? Maybe? But he wouldn't have had long. How long would our perpetrator have needed? Was Melanie grabbed and then stashed unconscious somewhere? A lockup or car boot? Wouldn't need very long for that.

So, who else? Janet? She must have had a bit of a

temper. But then again she only found out about

Adam and Melanie at the party. If she had known

beforehand she wouldn't have got so mad later on.

Ok, next suspect? Marcus and Jonathon from the

bookies were both dead and 'available' which could

only mean they didn't commit anything forbidden

during their life-times. So cross them off the list.

Unless it was down to someone he had yet to

discover, there was only one other person on his

list, Jimmy Beckinsworth. Murray still had a

question mark by him. He may not be guilty but he

may have seen who was responsible? He would

have had no more time than Danny on the stall, he

should already have been in work. Surely the

electrical shop would have opened at nine? Unfortunately the shop no longer existed. The phone started ringing on the desk next to Murray.

"Murray, it's me."

"Yes Jeff. Anything?"

"He's locked up! Quite a list of previous. Arson, shop-lifting. Then it's gets interesting. Attempted rape and rape. He turned into quite a nasty creature by the time he reached thirty. He's been on the sex offenders register for years. Repeat offender too so he won't be let out again now. He could well be your guy."

"I'd say! Do you think I could get to see him?"

"Would you really want to?" Jeff sounded unsure.

"How else am I going to find out where Melanie is? If he took her he's the only one who knows where she is now." Jeff thought for a minute.

"Ok, I'll see what I can do but no promises."

"I know. Thanks."

Jeff and Murray were shown into a small room with a table and chairs. There were cameras in two corners with red lights flashing. Everything was being recorded.

"Are you sure about this Murray?" Jeff asked looking at his friend.

"You keep asking me that! We're here now, let's get this over with." As the two of them sat down, a guard brought in a middle-aged man in hand-cuffs and told him to sit down across the table form Jeff and Murray. He then stood back against the door.

"Mr Beckinsworth?" Jeff started.

"Yes. They told me why you are here. I don't have anything to say." Murray studied the prematurely grey man in glasses. He looked clean and neat.

"Did you kill Melanie Foskett?" He asked it straight out in a monotone voice.

"Melanie Foskett?" The man stared at Murray and then up at the ceiling. "Melanie Foskett?" He repeated the name slowly.

"1974 if it helps your memory." Jeff spoke.

"How many have you murdered? Is it that hard to recall?" Murray was feeling anger rise up inside him. Or maybe it was rising inside Adam?

"1974 is a long time ago." Jimmy stared back down at Murray. "I do remember her. She was a lovely girl, long blonde hair, very pretty."

"Did you kill her?" Murray spoke flatly again.

Jimmy cocked his head on one side as if he was trying to decide whether he had or not. I went home sick that day. I wasn't well." He still stared at Murray.

"What time did you go home sick?" This time it was Jeff again.

"Just about the time Melanie arrived to go in to work." A smirk was now on Jimmy's face. "You'll never prove I had anything to do with her disappearance. You can't even prove she's dead."

"Her mother is now an old lady. She would like some closure." Jeff spoke softly. Jimmy turned his gaze towards the C.I.D. man.

"My mother's an old lady too. I wouldn't like to upset her."

"You did murder her didn't you?" Murray was

138

calm now, almost resigned to the outcome. "Where is she?"

"I've said all I'm going to say. Time for me to return to my room I think. Guard, I want to leave now."

CHAPTER THIRTEEN

They had driven most of the way back in silence. It was only as they neared home that Murray turned to his friend and asked.

"Do you have his mother's name and address?"

"Was it in the file?"

"No. Jimmy wasn't even named in the file."

"Oh, then no I'd say. Do you think she'll know something about this?"

"Maybe. Even if she does she probably won't talk." Murray felt dejection setting in. Would he ever be able to find Melanie's remains? "I might do a bit of searching when I get in."

"Good luck." Jeff offered as he pulled up outside Murray's flat. As Murray opened the car door Jeff's mobile rang, it was Kate. "Look's like it might be time? Hi honey, how... yeah, yeah... ok, I'm on my way.... love you." He hung it up and turned to Murray. "Well wish me luck then!"

"Go have a baby Friend!" Murray got out of the car and waved as Jeff drove off.

Back once again at his computer desk, Murray searched the birth certificate of James Beckinsworth. Hopefully from that he could get his mother's name. It was the only avenue left. He found what he wanted and switched his search to Lesley Beckinsworth. Nothing. Not again. He couldn't call on Jeff this time either.

He decided he was going to take a break. He picked up his keys and drove west. He pulled into the town's car park and strolled down to the quay again. Fowey was looking as picturesque as the last time he visited. He sat and took in the tourists, the boats bobbing around on the river and the seagulls which were flying around in the bright blue sky above his head. He didn't want to end this case like this. Left up in the air. Poor Mrs Foskett not knowing the last resting place of her daughter. He thought that maybe he should pay her a visit while he was in town. He phoned ahead to make sure it was ok. It was.

He was once again shown into the conservatory. The frail looking Catherine Foskett beamed at her returning guest. He asked how she was and about what she had been up to. She chatted away but it didn't take her long to get around to the subject of her daughter.

".. Now come on young man, you've not come here just to say hello. Have you found out anything about Melanie?" She was searching his eyes for some clue as to whether he had good news or bad.

"I think I know who hurt Melanie, Mrs Foskett. But I can't prove it, not yet."

"Who?" She was still staring into his eyes. He wanted to look away but couldn't.

"A young man called Jimmy Beckinsworth. He's in prison now. He's hurt other girls..."

"Jimmy? From the electric store? Lesley's boy?"

"You knew his mother?" Maybe there was hope still?

"Lesley, yes. She's gone now. Cancer I think it was... He always seemed such a nice quiet, polite boy... Destroys your trust in anyone doesn't it?" She sat back in her chair and stared out at the river.

"I'm sorry." Murray muttered. "I want to find where he put her. I thought perhaps the mother would be able to help. He said she was still alive?"

"No." Catherine was shaking her head slowly. "She died a few years back now I'm sure, positive."

Murray left the elderly lady with her thoughts and headed back to his car. Now he needed Ali and Rita to find Mrs Lesley Beckinsworth....

CHAPTER FOURTEEN

An excited Jeff finally phoned with the good news at a quarter to eleven that night. He was now the proud father of a beautiful little girl. Jessica Elizabeth had weighed in at seven pounds nine ounces. Both mother and baby were just fine even if daddy was still shaking like a leaf!

Murray poured himself a glass of wine and called

Jenny with the good news. She was thrilled for Jeff

and Kate if not a little wary about the impending

Godparent bit. Still, they must go and visit as soon

as possible.

Murray relaxed on his sofa after he hung up the

phone. It was exciting. Maybe he felt a little left

behind in the 'growing up' stakes but he always

knew that married life and babies would make the

'other side' of his life very complicated, like it wasn't

already!

He downed his drink and considered an early

night when a strange voice spoke to him from the

corner of the room.

"Mr Murray Barber?" the woman's voice asked.

"Erm.. yes. Who are you?" he stared around the

lounge and rested his gaze on the corner where the voice came from.

"I think you know who I am. You want me to help you." It was a statement, not a question. Murray thought for a moment. Could it be her?

"Mrs Beckinsworth? Mrs Lesley Beckinsworth?" he asked cautiously.

"You'll find her in the basement. He was always so secretive about what he was up to down there. She must be there."

"You're talking about Melanie?" he asked quietly as if he might scare the woman away.

"I don't know why he turned out like he did. I suppose it must be my fault. Isn't that what they always say? I don't know what happened to her. I don't know what he did. I don't know why he did what he did."

"I'm sorry he put you through this Mrs Beckinsworth."

"Bishops Row. Number three. She must be in the basement." Murray waited for more but something told him the woman had gone. He sat back down on his settee and slowly pulled his notebook towards him. He jotted down the address she had given him. The road wasn't very far away. He knew it quite well. Had she always been that close?

He hadn't called anyone that night. He had opened another bottle of wine and drank the lot and then fallen asleep on the settee. The next morning he ignored the phone which was showing a strange number and let it switch to answerphone. It was another job by the sound of it. It could wait. He

called his Aunt Pam and filled her in on all that had

happened. She was thoughtful as though aware that

he was finding it all a bit overwhelming and

upsetting. After all, it wasn't everyday you

considered what happened on the last day of your

last life! She did tell him that he must report it. Yes,

Jeff was now off on paternity leave, but he would

know the best person to pass the case onto. It must

be done. Melanie needed to be found and her

remains laid to rest.

  He did manage to get through to Jeff who was still

bouncing off the walls with excitement. Jeff took in

the details that Murray told him and said he would

deal with it. He'd also pass on Murray's number so

that the officer could keep him informed. It may

take a while, they didn't even know who now lived in the house. Jeff then went on to invite both Murray and Jenny along to the hospital that evening to meet his new daughter. Murray gladly accepted the invite.

During the day Murray accepted his next case, and another one that called after lunch, but he found it hard to get his mind focused on them. He arranged to pick Jenny up at six and they would head straight to the hospital. She told him that he should leave it to her to pick up gifts for the new parents and baby. This set Murray wondering if this experience would push Jenny into the 'broody' mode that seemed to overtake women when they got around all things 'baby'? Would he start to feel pressurized into settling down to a family life? A very complicated family life? And where would that leave Michelle? He had shaken his head, he wasn't ready for all that yet. Life may go on, but not at a pace he couldn't keep up with.

Jenny was ready and waiting for him when he pulled up outside her house-share at six o'clock. She loaded the gifts, already wrapped with ribbons and bows, into the back seat.

"I've bought a hand-knitted shawl for Jessica and had her name sewn onto it. I've bought a cigar for Jeff, very traditional! And I've got Kate some lavender candles, they're supposed to be very calming."

"Oh, great! Sounds good. Are you ready for this?"

"Yes, let's get this over with."

They drove to the hospital and were let through the

security doors into the maternity wing. Murray felt a little like he was back at the prison. Kate looked tired but happy. Jeff just looked like a kid in a sweet shop! The baby was tiny, wrapped in a soft pink baby blanket.

They all 'oohed' and 'aahed' but it wasn't Jenny who had a life-changing experience when she took her turn in holding the baby... It was Murray. With the nerves of holding such a precious armful ricocheting throughout his body, he suddenly felt that this was what life was really all about. Studying the tiny perfect features of the gurgling bundle in his arms, all the cliché sayings he had ever heard about new parents, made all the sense in the world. He glanced across at Jenny. Would she become the mother of their own tiny miracle?

CHAPTER FIFTEEN

It was nearly two weeks later that Murray was
informed about the discovery in the basement at
number three Bishops Row. He had expected to
hear something but it still shook him to hear the
words. Jeff took him down to the morgue once the
forensics were finished, he was shown a table where
a selection of bones were respectfully laid out. A few
strands of matted long blonde hair and some
tattered straps of cloth, some a dark brown, the
others pale with a few flecks of orange. Murray
hadn't generally been an emotional man but he had
let a tear slide down his cheek.

Mrs Catherine Foskett had been informed as well. She in turn had invited Murray to the belated funeral of her daughter. He asked if it would be alright to inform the Cannon-Leigh family, it was. Melanie was finally to be laid to rest next to her father in an informal private service. Her remains had been too decomposed for any definite cause of death to be confirmed.

Murray had asked Jenny to accompany him. She didn't know how deep his feelings went about the case, or why. She herself had no true idea who Melanie was but still she sniffled through the short service.

Murray had been doing some hard thinking in the time since Jessica's birth. If he really wanted to move forward with his life, this life, the life of

Murray Barber, then he had decisions to make. And made them he had.

He had arranged to go over and see Michelle at her home. Her nice terraced house that hid the extensive redecorated interior. He had broken her heart. She hadn't said he had done so but he could see it clearly written across her face as he ended their affair. She had remained calm and together as she leaned against her kitchen side, arms folded tightly across her chest. Her eyes refusing to meet his but instead reaching no higher than his chest. Her lack of emotion was worse than if she had screamed and hit out at him. He had felt wretched. He felt totally responsible. But he had to do it. She had repeated how it had always been a casual affair with no strings attached. He had told her it was

Jenny who he really loved. Jenny with her imaginative mind and ever-changing hair colour and her blind willingness to stay oblivious to his crazy life. Had Michelle collapsed in devastation when he closed the door behind him as he left for the last time? He didn't know.

And it was with Jenny that he now stood. Silently mourning the death of Melanie and the loss of his past existence, if that was what it had been. This was marking the end of a personal episode. A new story lay ahead, waiting for him. The rest of the life of Murray Barber.

The service was solemn and short. Most of the grieving had long since been over. The sun continued shining and as Catherine Foskett said her thankyou's and returned to her nursing home, Murray suggested he and Jenny take a stroll through the town. They headed up along the road following the river's edge to where they reached the small sandy cove, arriving just as most bathers were packing up and heading back into town and home for tea. They walked down to the water's edge and watched the waves gently lapping over their feet. Murray turned to Jenny and studied her face, taking in her every furrow and freckle. She was beautiful, no matter what colour her hair was.

  "Jenny?" he whispered.

  "It's lovely here isn't it." she smiled up at him.

  "Not as lovely as you."

  "Oh shut up! Not like you to be so romantic."

  "Jenny?" His voice was soft and quiet.

"What?" she kept his gaze this time.

"Will you marry me?"

Jenny studied him for what seemed like hours but in reality, was no more than seconds. Was he serious?

"Oh Murray..... No!"